Happy Fell

by Erica S. Perl

illustrated by Chris Chatterton

Penguin Workshop

PENGUIN WORKSHOP
An Imprint of Penguin Random House LLC, New York

Text copyright © 2019 by Erica S. Perl. Illustrations copyright © 2019 by Penguin Random House LLC. All rights reserved. Published by Penguin Workshop, an imprint of Penguin Random House LLC, New York. PENGUIN and PENGUIN WORKSHOP are trademarks of Penguin Books Ltd, and the W colophon is a registered trademark of Penguin Random House LLC. Manufactured in China.

Library of Congress Cataloging-in-Publication Data is available upon request.

Visit us online at www.penguinrandomhouse.com.

ISBN 9781524790455 (paperback)   10 9 8 7 6 5 4 3 2 1
ISBN 9781524790462 (library binding)   10 9 8 7 6 5 4 3 2 1

To Bougie. I can't help felling in love
with you—ESP

Chapter One

"Arnold! Come quick!" called Louise.

Arnold ran outside. "What's up?"

"Leaves!" said Louise.

"Except they're not *up* anymore. They're down, all around. See? That means it's finally fell. Happy fell, Arnold!"

Arnold scratched his head. "Don't you mean *fall*?"

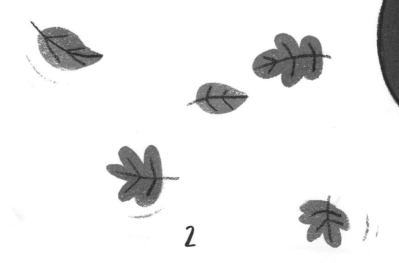

Louise laughed. "No, silly. Fall already happened. Fall was when the leaves turned color. *Fell* is the season when the leaves are on the ground. And today is the first day of fell!"

"I'm not sure fell is a real

season," said Arnold.

"Oh, it's real, all right," said Louise. "And it calls for a celebration."

"It does?" asked Arnold.

"It does," said Louise.

Just then, Arnold had a great idea.

So did Louise.

Together, they said, "We should make—"

"—the biggest leaf pile in the world!" said Louise.

"—my famous sticky popcorn balls," said Arnold.

"Popcorn balls?" Louise looked confused. "But it's perfect leaf-pile weather!"

A chilly breeze made the leaves dance. It also made Arnold shiver.

Arnold looked at his cozy cottage.

"You go ahead," he told Louise.

"You're not going to help?" asked Louise.

"Maybe later," said Arnold. "Right now, it's popcorn-ball time."

"Great idea!" said Louise.
"I will help you, then you will
help me!"

"Oh, that's okay—" Arnold
started to say.

But Louise was already in
the kitchen.

"What should I do first?" she
asked.

Chapter Two

"First, you melt the butter," read Arnold. "Next, you mix the melted butter with brown sugar. Then, you pop the popcorn."

Louise tried to melt the butter.

"Oops!"

"It's okay," said Arnold.

Then she tried to scoop the

sugar.

14

"Oops!"

"It's okay," said Arnold.

"Look, Arnold! I'm mixing
them together," Louise called
as she slid by.

"Not okay!" Arnold grabbed

the table to steady himself.

17

He filled a bucket with
soapy water and got a mop.
"Keep an eye on the
popcorn while I clean this up,"
he told Louise.

19

He was almost finished

when he heard another "Oops!"

"Louise, I told you to keep

an eye on the—"

"—POPCORN."

"Wheee!"

"Try it, Arnold," said Louise.

"It's just like a leaf pile."

"New plan," said Arnold,

guiding his sticky, popcorn-

covered friend to the door.

"Let's go outside and make

that leaf pile."

"Really? Right now?" said
Louise.

"Right now," said Arnold.

Chapter Three

Outside, Arnold and Louise gathered leaves.

"Look, Arnold. Our leaf pile is bigger than me!" said Louise.

"So, we're done?" asked
Arnold.

"Of course not! It needs to
be the biggest leaf pile in the
world!"

Arnold raked more. And more. And more.

Arnold raked like Arnold did everything: slowly and carefully.

Louise tried to wait, but—

FWOOSH!

"Louise!" said Arnold. "Now
we have to start over."

Arnold started over, slowly
and carefully.

Louise did, too, and then—

FWOOSH!

"Louise, stop jumping!" said Arnold, putting down his rake.

"I can't!" said Louise, giggling. "It's too much fun. You try!"

"I don't want to jump," said Arnold. "I want to go back inside. I want to make popcorn balls."

"But what about our leaf pile?" asked Louise.

"I tried to make a leaf pile—
twice! Both times, you ruined it
before I could finish."

Louise jumped again. This
time, in frustration.

"Ruined?" she said. "I was just testing it out, that's all."

"It doesn't need testing," replied Arnold. "It needs finishing."

"You know what, Arnold?" said Louise. "I don't think I need your help after all."

"Great!" said Arnold. "I will go inside and make popcorn balls. By myself."

35

"Super!" said Louise. "I will stay outside and make the world's biggest leaf pile. By myself."

Chapter Four

Back in his kitchen, Arnold

melted butter.

Slowly.

He measured and poured

sugar.

Carefully.

He stirred the mixture and popped popcorn into a big bowl.

Very slowly and carefully.

Arnold smiled. Everything was going perfectly perfect.

Except . . .

One important ingredient was missing: messy, sticky, unstoppable . . .

Louise.

Outside, Louise gathered leaves.

She stacked them in a big, messy pile.

She added more and made an even bigger and messier pile.

Then more and more until it was possibly the biggest leaf pile in the world.

And definitely the messiest.

Louise smiled. Everything was going perfectly perfect.

Except . . .

One important thing

was missing: slow, careful,

thoughtful . . .

Arnold.

Chapter Five

Arnold did not like to rush.

(Rushing made things messy,

and Arnold hated messy.)

But right now he had to rush.

Even if it meant that he would

get a little messy.

As everything came together,

Arnold began to smile.

It was the perfect surprise

for Louise.

Louise was rushing, too.

(Rushing was her favorite.)

But she kept dropping

things, so she tried to slow

down.

You need to be careful,

like Arnold, she told herself.

As everything came together,

Louise jumped for joy.

It was the perfect surprise

for Arnold.

Soon, Arnold heard a knock
at his door.

knock
knock

"Just a minute!" he called.

His hands were sticky.

His apron was sticky, too.

There was another knock at the door.

"Coming!" called Arnold, balancing his tray.

He tried to open the door, but it wouldn't budge.

"Hang on," said Arnold. "The door is stuck, and so am I."

49

Arnold tried to pull. Louise tried to push.

No luck. Still stuck.

"Try again, on three," said
Arnold. "One . . . two . . . three!"

Arnold gave an extra-big tug.

Louise gave an extra-big push.

Whoa!!!

"Oh no!" cried Louise. "My surprise for you is ruined!"

"My surprise for you is . . ." Arnold started to laugh. "On your head."

Louise reached up and began to laugh, too. "Is it a hat?"

Arnold shook his head. "I made you my famous sticky popcorn balls. Did you bring me the biggest leaf pile in the world?"

Louise nodded.

"I love it," said Arnold.

"Thank you, Louise."

"Thank you, Arnold. I'm sorry for messing everything up."

"It's okay," said Arnold. "I'm just glad we can still celebrate the first day of fell together."

"You are?" Louise was surprised. "I thought you didn't believe in fell."

"I didn't used to," admitted

Arnold. "But then I kind of fell into it."

"That's the way it is with fell. It's sort of like brr," said Louise.

"Brr? What's brr?" asked Arnold.

Louise rolled her eyes.

"Brr is the season between fell and winter," she said. "Don't you remember, Arnold? We always have fun in brr!"

"I do remember now," said
Arnold. "And I can hardly
wait."